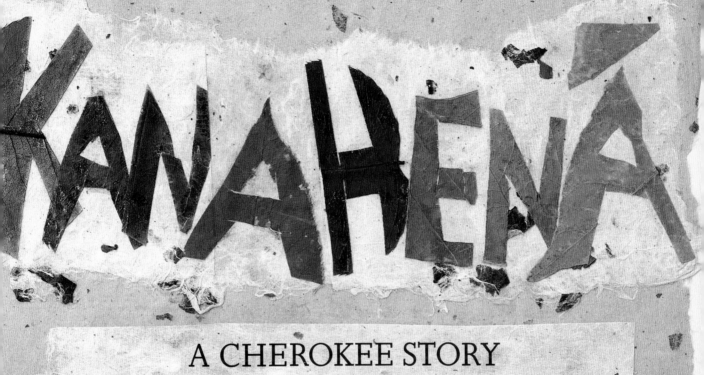

KANAHENA

A CHEROKEE STORY

Susan L. Roth

ST. MARTIN'S PRESS   New York

Acknowledgments
I would like to thank Victor Golla, Jean Karl, Eva Laufer,
Cesare Marino, Ruth Phang, AAA and J. Roth, Ed and
Kay Sharpe, Mercedes Tibbits, Janet Vultee, Dee Yanni.

Based on a Cherokee story called
"The Terrapin's Escape from the Wolves."

Library of Congress Cataloging-in-Publication Data

Roth, Susan L.
Kanahéna.

Summary: A retelling of the traditional Cherokee tale of Terrapin the trickster and how he
outwitted the Bad Wolf and the Other Wolves.
1. Cherokee Indians—Legends—Juvenile literature.
2. Indians of the North American—Appalachian Mountains, Southern—Legends—Juvenile
literature. [1. Cherokee Indians—Legends. 2. Indians of North America—Legends]
I. Title.
E99.C5R85   1987   398.2'08997 [E]   87–43203
ISBN 0-312-01722-7

to JR, love, SR,
grazie a Lei—

The old woman was cooking, stirring a hanging pot on an open fire, stirring something yellow, grainy, soupy.

"What are you making?" the little girl asked her. "What's in your pot?"

"Kanahéna. Real Kanahéna," the old woman said. "No one makes it now, no one but me. I am the oldest in the village. I remember when my mother cooked Kanahéna for me, on this fire, at this very place, when I was young like you. Kanahéna is the real food of the Cherokees. Come sit with me, child, not too close to the fire. I'll let you taste my Kanahéna and I'll tell you a story about Kanahéna and Terrapin. It's an old Cherokee story, about an old Cherokee food. Hominy, you could call it, or cornmeal mush, the oldest old Cherokee food."

The little girl sat.

"Do you even know what a terrapin is? They don't call things by their proper names anymore."

"It's a turtle." The little girl knew.

"Well," said the old woman, "then I'll tell you the story. It's an old-time story. The animals could talk then."

"Oh," said the child, and she crossed her legs and waited.

Terrapin and Possum went looking for persimmons.

Possum climbed.

He threw persimmons down to Terrapin.

Bad Wolf came along. He jumped in front of
Terrapin and ate the persimmons just as fast as
Possum threw them.

But Possum tricked Bad Wolf. He threw the biggest
persimmon of all. Bad Wolf tried to eat that persimmon too.
But it was so big that it got stuck in Bad Wolf's throat.
Bad Wolf choked.

"I'll take Bad Wolf's ears for Kanahéna spoons," said Terrapin.

Terrapin left Possum eating persimmons in the persimmon
tree and went on. As he walked along the road he stopped
to visit a friend.

"Have some Kanahéna," invited his friend.

"Thank you," said Terrapin. Terrapin used Bad Wolf's ears
for spoons to eat the Kanahéna.

Strange, thought Terrapin's friend, strange.

Terrapin went on. As he walked along the road he stopped
to visit another friend.

"Have some Kanahéna," invited his friend.

"Thank you," said Terrapin. And again Terrapin used Bad
Wolf's ears for spoons to eat the Kanahéna.

Strange, thought Terrapin's friend, strange.

Strange news travels quickly.

The Other Wolves heard that Bad Wolf had choked and that Terrapin had taken his ears. They heard that Terrapin was eating Kanahéna at his friends' houses, using Bad Wolf's ears for spoons. The Other Wolves were furious.

The Other Wolves followed Terrapin as he went on visiting his friends and eating Kanahéna with Bad Wolf's ears for spoons. And soon the Other Wolves caught Terrapin.

"We shall boil you in a clay pot," said the Other Wolves, "You deserve that for your bad behavior."

"Ha-ha-ha," laughed Terrapin. "I'll kick your pot all to pieces."

"Then we'll roast you on a fire," said the Other Wolves.
"You deserve that for your bad behavior."
"Ha-ha-ha," laughed Terrapin. "I'll blow your fire out."

"Then we'll throw you into the deepest part of the river, where you will drown," said the Other Wolves.

"Oh, no, not THAT!" begged Terrapin. "Not the deep, deep water! Not the river!"

The Other Wolves had no mercy for Terrapin. They threw him into the deepest part of the river.

But Terrapin had tricked the Other Wolves. The deep water was just where he wanted to be. He was a good swimmer. He came up on the other side of the river, and escaped from the Other Wolves.

Some say that Terrapin hit his back on a rock in the river, and broke his shell in many pieces. Some say he sang an old Cherokee medicine song to heal himself:

Gu daye wu, Gu daye wu,
I have sewed myself together,
I have sewed myself together.

They say his shell grew back together, but that the scars are still there to this day.

"Did you like the Cherokee story?" asked the old woman.

"Yes," said the child, "but did Bad Wolf die?"

"Maybe he just lost his ears, that old Bad Wolf," said the woman. "What about your Kanahéna? It's ready to eat now."

"All right," said the little girl. "But I want to eat with a regular spoon."

Kanahéna

You can make your own Kanahéna with this recipe. You will need:

 1 grown-up to help you
 2 cups water
 1 cup cornmeal
 1 teaspoon salt
 a little more cold water

Let the two cups of plain water boil in a pot, add salt. Wet the cornmeal with the extra cold water. Add the wet meal slowly to the boiling water, and stir until it is done.

   This is the way that Cherokee people ate their Kanahéna. You may try it this way, or you may prefer to try it with:

 melted butter on top,
     or,
 small pieces of cheese stirred into the Kanahéna while it is hot,
     or,
 honey, jelly, or jam,
     or,
 whatever sounds good to you.

Kha - lih - **sta** - y

ᏣᎳᎩ ᎠᏕᎶ

Let's eat.